Dear Parents:

Congratulations! Your child is taking the first steps on an exciting journey. The destination? Independent reading!

STEP INTO READING® will help your child get there. The program offers five steps to reading success. Each step includes fun stories and colorful art or photographs. In addition to original fiction and books with favorite characters, there are Step into Reading Non-Fiction Readers, Phonics Readers and Boxed Sets, Sticker Readers, and Comic Readers—a complete literacy program with something to interest every child.

Learning to Read, Step by Step!

Ready to Read   Preschool–Kindergarten
• big type and easy words • rhyme and rhythm • picture clues
For children who know the alphabet and are eager to begin reading.

Reading with Help   Preschool–Grade 1
• basic vocabulary • short sentences • simple stories
For children who recognize familiar words and sound out new words with help.

Reading on Your Own   Grades 1–3
• engaging characters • easy-to-follow plots • popular topics
For children who are ready to read on their own.

Reading Paragraphs   Grades 2–3
• challenging vocabulary • short paragraphs • exciting stories
For newly independent readers who read simple sentences with confidence.

Ready for Chapters   Grades 2–4
• chapters • longer paragraphs • full-color art
For children who want to take the plunge into chapter books but still like colorful pictures.

STEP INTO READING® is designed to give every child a successful reading experience. The grade levels are only guides; children will progress through the steps at their own speed, developing confidence in their reading. The F&P Text Level on the back cover serves as another tool to help you choose the right book for your child.

Remember, a lifetime love of reading starts with a single step!

For Carlos Tapia
—E.W. and M.F.

To my family
—A.G.

Text copyright © 2012 by Ellen Weiss and Mel Friedman
Cover art and interior illustrations copyright © 2012 by Alessia Girasole

Published in the United States by Random House Children's Books, a division of Penguin Random House LLC, New York.

Step into Reading, Random House, and the Random House colophon are registered trademarks of Penguin Random House LLC.

Visit us on the Web!
StepIntoReading.com
randomhousekids.com

Educators and librarians, for a variety of teaching tools, visit us at
RHTeachersLibrarians.com

Library of Congress Cataloging-in-Publication Data
Weiss, Ellen.
The stinky giant / by Ellen Weiss and Mel Friedman ; illustrated by Alessia Girasole.
    p. cm. — (Step into reading. A step 3 book)
Summary: Pepper and Jake, sister and brother shepherds, match wits with the giant, Urk, who regularly floods their valley with his dirty washwater.
ISBN 978-0-375-86743-9 (trade) — ISBN 978-0-375-96743-6 (lib. bdg.) —
ISBN 978-0-375-98344-3 (ebook)
[1. Giants—Fiction. 2. Riddles—Fiction. 3. Brothers and sisters—Fiction. 4. Shepherds—Fiction.]
I. Friedman, Mel. II. Girasole, Alessia, ill. III. Title.
PZ7.W4472Sti 2012   [E]—dc22   2010035397

Printed in the United States of America
10 9 8 7 6

This book has been officially leveled by using the F&P Text Level Gradient™ Leveling System.

Random House Children's Books supports the First Amendment and celebrates the right to read.

STEP INTO READING®

3

STEP

READING ON YOUR OWN

The Stinky Giant

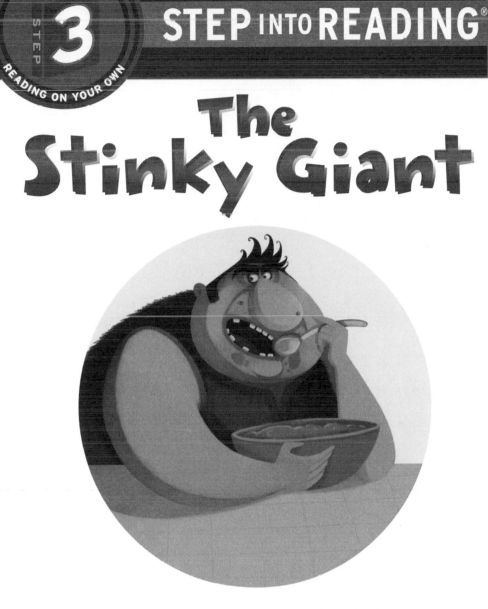

by Ellen Weiss and Mel Friedman

illustrated by Alessia Girasole

Random House 🏠 New York

A long time ago,

a brother and sister lived

in a beautiful valley.

The sister's name was Pepper.

The brother's name was Jake.

They had a happy life.

Every day, they sang songs

and watched their sheep.

They only had one problem.

The problem's name was Urk.

Urk was a huge, mean giant.

He was rude.

He was ugly.

When Urk burped,
it sounded like thunder.
When he sneezed,
houses blew away.

Urk lived in a castle.
It was way, way, way up
on top of the mountain.

Every Thursday,

Urk washed his clothes.

Urk's clothes were very big.

Urk's washtub was very big, too.

When he was done
washing his clothes,
Urk emptied his washtub.
The water came roaring
down the mountain.
It made a huge flood.

Sometimes things were swept away.
Sometimes some of Pepper and Jake's
sheep were lost.

So Pepper and Jake had to walk
way down the valley
to get their sheep back.
Pepper and Jake were tired
of Urk and Urk's laundry.

One day,

Jake fell into a big puddle

of Urk's dirty wash water.

He came out all stinky.

"That's it.

We are going to talk to Urk,"

said Jake.

They looked up at Urk's castle.

It would be hard to get there.

But they knew they had to go.

So they made some

egg-and-salty-pickle sandwiches.

They filled a goatskin bag

with water.

And they set out

to climb Urk's mountain.

They climbed up, up, up.

The higher they went,
the colder it got.
Their teeth chattered.
Their sweat froze.

After a while,

they got hungry.

They stopped to eat

their sandwiches.

Their lunch made them thirsty.

But the water in the goatskin

was frozen solid.

Finally,

they arrived at the castle.

They banged hard on the door.

The door swung open.

There, sitting at his table,

was Urk.

He was having a gigantic

bowl of smelly soup.

"Well,"

said the giant,

"what do you want?"

"We want you to stop flooding us
with your dirty wash water,"
said Pepper.
The giant's laughter boomed
across the room.

But Jake and Pepper

scowled at him

so he would know

how serious they were.

Urk just kept laughing.

"Okay,"

Urk finally said.

"I have an idea.

We giants have a secret riddle.

No one has ever been able

to answer it.

"If you can't answer the riddle,

I will boil you for soup.

And I will throw

your sheep in, too.

If you can answer it, I lose.

I will move away."

"Where will you move to?"
asked Pepper.
"You can pick,
because I won't lose,"
said Urk.

Jake pointed to the map.

"Here,"

he said.

They shook on it.

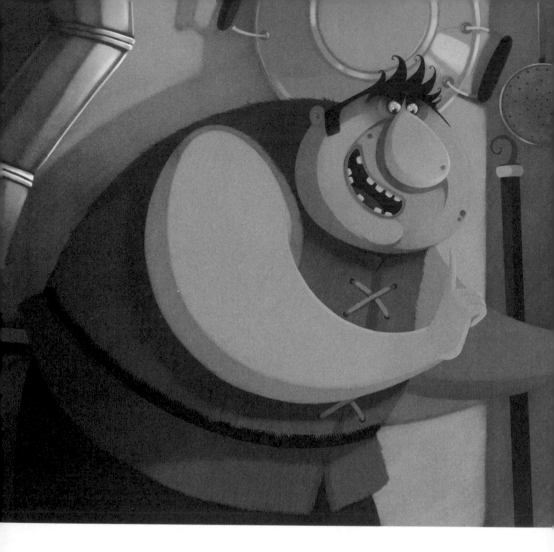

Urk gave them the riddle.
"There is something
you see every day,
and it is one thing
but also three things.

"I will give you three days
to come up with the answer!"
shouted the giant.
"Now go home!"

Pepper and Jake went
down, down, down the mountain.

"Look," said Pepper.

"The ice in the bag

has turned back to water."

Jake was so thirsty,

he drank half the water.

When they finally got home,
they started thinking
about the riddle.
What could be one thing
but three things?
They only had three days,
or they would be
Jake-and-Pepper-and-sheep soup!

"What about a fish?" Pepper said.

"First it's an egg, then it's a fish—"

"And that's all," said Jake.

"Two things."

On the second day,

Jake had an idea.

"Peanut butter!"

he said.

"It's crunchy, or it's creamy—"

"And that's all,"

said Pepper.

Then she said,

"What about a book?

It's open or it's closed—"

But that was only two things.

After that, they were so tired,

they had to go to sleep.

But they went to bed scared.

If they didn't come up

with an answer tomorrow,

they would be soup!

On the third morning,

Jake and Pepper

were really worried.

Today they had to go back to Urk.

And they still had no answer.

"Let's have some dandelion tea,"
said Pepper.
"It will help us think."
So Jake put water in the kettle
and put the kettle on to boil.

Pepper decided she would have
some iced tea.

Soon the water was boiling.

The kettle whistled.

The steam came jetting

out of the spout.

Jake and Pepper looked at the steam.

They looked at Pepper's ice.

Then they looked at each other.

"Water!"

they said together.

Water, like the stuff
they used to make the tea!

Water, like the ice
in Pepper's glass!

Urk hated it,

but a deal was a deal.

He left the very next day

for the Horrible Land of Hooey.

But he left

his dirty socks behind.

And water, like the steam
coming out of the kettle!

They raced back up the mountain.
They didn't even care that
the water in their goatskin bag
was turning to ice.
And they didn't even care about
Urk's steamy, stinky wash water.
They had won.

"We figured it out!" said Pepper.

"It's water!" said Jake.

"Steam, ice, and liquid!

But all water!"

Urk turned red.

Then he turned purple.

"No!" he shouted.

"You couldn't have figured

that out!

Nobody figures it out!"

But they had.

And a deal was a deal.

Urk would have to move
to the Horrible Land of Hooey.
And he would have to wash
his clothes
in the Great Smelly Swamp.